THE

Treasure

SADDLEBACK
PUBLISHING

T H E   H E I G H T S™

Blizzard	Ransom
Camp	River
Crash	Sail
Creature	Score
Dam	Shelter
Dive	Swamp
Heist	**Treasure**
Jump	Tsunami
Mudslide	Twister
Neptune	Wild

Original text by Ed Hansen
Adapted by Mary Kate Doman

SADDLEBACK
P U B L I S H I N G
www.sdlback.com

ISBN-13: 978-1-62250-048-2
ISBN-10: 1-62250-048-2
eBook: 978-1-61247-706-0

Printed in Guangzhou, China
NOR/0713/CA21301277

17 16 15 14 13   2 3 4 5 6 7

Chapter 1

Todd Bardo Jr. walked across the
Penn State campus. He was lost
in thought. He was thinking about
South America.

Todd was a well-liked junior
in college. His roommate and best
friend was Franco Silva. Franco and
Todd were football players. Now that
the season was over, they had a lot of
free time.

Franco and Todd met for lunch in the cafeteria. Franco got there first and waited. When Todd sat down, he put his head on the table.

"What's wrong?" asked Franco.

"I am stressed," Todd said. "You know I was born in Ecuador. My dad was a doctor. After medical school, he went to South America. He went to help the poor for a month. But he ended up staying there for forty years."

"Yeah, I remember you telling me about your dad. He was a respected doctor," Franco said.

"Yes, he was. Most of his patients were poor. He never charged anyone a lot. He asked them to pay what they could," said Todd. "He got paid in fruit, vegetables, chickens … Everyone loved and respected him. He even built a clinic in Quito, the capital."

"Why does that make you stressed?" Franco said.

"After my dad retired, the government wanted to thank him. They gave him exclusive salvage rights to five miles of reef. The Ecuadorian government did that for people who helped their country."

"That's awesome. Did you ever dive on the reef?" asked Franco.

"No. After my dad died, I inherited the salvage rights. But only for five years. This is the fifth year. I need to set up a diving trip now. My rights are set to expire," Todd explained.

He continued, "Ecuador has the safest harbor in South America. Guayaquil is a deepwater port that's centuries old. There's a bunch of reefs offshore. These reefs aren't dangerous now. But hundreds of ships were wrecked during Spanish rule. These old ships usually carried gold, silver, and jewels. I could be a millionaire!"

"So? Set up a diving trip. It sounds like fun," said Franco.

"I can't," Todd went on. "I can dive, just like you. But I don't have a clue about salvage work. And it costs a lot of money."

"Wow!" Franco exclaimed. "Now I know why you're so worried. I think I know someone who can help."

"Really?" Todd asked. "Who?"

"My dad," Franco replied. "He was a salvage diver in the navy."

"No way!" Todd said.

"Yeah. I'm going home this weekend. Come with me," Franco said. "You can tell my dad about your salvage rights. I bet he'd love to help!"

Chapter 2

Franco and Todd went to Rockdale Heights that Friday.

"Dad, Todd has a problem. I thought you might be able to help him," said Franco.

"I'll try," said Rafael. "What's going on, Todd?"

Todd explained his problem with the salvage rights.

"That's a great problem," Rafael said. "You're very lucky."

"Oh, there's one more thing," Todd said. "Half of what I find goes to the government of Ecuador. I'll split the other half with anyone who helps me."

Rafael wanted to hear more of Todd's story. He looked interested.

"I've Googled the reefs," Todd continued. "Several ships sank on my five-mile stretch. Last year a man found over three million dollars in gold. His salvage rights were only ten miles south of mine."

"It looks like you have something here. And I want to help," Rafael said. "I have a friend in Florida. We go diving together. If he joined us, we'd have four divers. That's a perfect salvage team."

"But it's going to cost a lot of money," Todd said. "And I can't afford it."

"Well, what if I pay our expenses? We'll take these costs out of any treasure we find. Then, after we pay the government, we'll divide what's left. Todd, they're your diving rights. You should get most of the money. At least fifty-five percent of what's left. Then we'll divide the rest. Fair?" asked Rafael.

"Yes. I think your plan is perfect," Todd exclaimed.

"Great, I'll give my friend Jorge a call," Rafael said. "If he's in, I'll set up the dive for June."

That night Rafael called Jorge. He was in. Everything was set. The four divers would be looking for treasure in Ecuador.

"We have to go to Guayaquil as soon as we can," Rafael told the boys. "We have to check all the rules. Then we'll charter a boat. We also need to order our equipment. We have five months to get ready. But there's a lot to do!"

Chapter 3

Two weeks later Rafael and Todd
flew to Quito, Ecuador. They were
making plans for the diving trip in
June. Since Todd owned the salvage
rights, he needed to be there. Todd
would meet with government
officials. Rafael would reserve a
boat and diving equipment.

Rafael and Todd met with Señor
Perez, an Ecuadorian official. They

went over the details of the salvage rights.

"I knew your father well," Señor Perez said. "Dr. Bardo was a good man. I'm very happy you're here, Todd. I hope you find treasure."

"Thank you, Señor Perez," Todd said. "Can you recommend a boat captain to us?"

"My friend Miguel Sanchez has a boat. It's called the *Paz*," said Señor Perez. "It's perfect for your expedition. Captain Sanchez is honest and reliable."

"Thanks again," Todd replied. "I hope Captain Sanchez can help us."

Upon arriving in Guayaquil, they found the *Paz* easily. About fifty feet long, she was a strong boat. The

Paz had a large crane that could lift twenty tons. She also had a big open deck. The *Paz* was perfect for treasure diving.

The next day a deckhand led Rafael and Todd to the captain.

Captain Sanchez had dark hair. He was in his fifties. He looked like a boat captain. A big black dog was sitting next to him.

"Ahoy, gentlemen! Welcome aboard the *Paz*," Captain Sanchez said. "This is my dog, Amigo. What can I do for you?"

"This is Todd Bardo Jr. I'm Rafael Silva. Todd's late father had diving rights on the reef," Rafael said. "We want to charter your boat to dive this June."

"I've heard about your father. But I never met him. Everyone said he was a great man," Captain Sanchez said.

"Thank you, Captain," Todd said. "It's nice to hear good things about him. I miss him a lot."

Captain Sanchez looked at his calendar. The whole month of June was free. Rafael and Todd booked it. Then Rafael asked about renting diving equipment.

"You can get everything you need here," Captain Sanchez said. "Guayaquil has tanks, pumps, and explosives if you need them. And don't forget bang sticks! They will protect you from a shark attack.

Treasure diving has become a major industry here."

Rafael signed a contract and paid a deposit. Todd was very excited. His dream of salvaging the reef was happening!

Chapter 4

June came fast. Rafael, Franco, Todd,
and Jorge were finally on their way
to Quito!

"I don't want you guys to be upset
if we don't find anything. Think of
this trip as an adventure," Rafael
said. "If we do find treasure, it's an
added bonus!"

The five-hour drive from Quito

to Guayaquil seemed like forever. Everyone was very excited.

"*Hola!*" Captain Sanchez shouted. "My deckhand, Domingo, will help you bring your gear aboard."

Domingo led them to a cabin with four bunks. There was a locker for each diver too. Once everything was stowed, they went back on deck.

"I've been looking at the charts," Captain Sanchez said. "Your salvage area is fifteen miles north. It will take less than two hours to get there. Then we'll anchor and dive in. All of your equipment is here. Everything's ready to go. We can take off early tomorrow."

"Awesome!" Todd exclaimed.

The next day Todd was the first one up and on deck. He went into the wheelhouse as Captain Sanchez turned on the motor. Also known as the pilothouse, it contained all of the ship's controls.

"*Buenos días*, Todd," the captain said. "Are you ready for a day of diving?"

"I've been ready for a long time!" Todd said.

Everyone met and ate breakfast on deck.

"We'll dive in teams," Rafael said. "Franco will dive with me. And Todd and Jorge will dive together. First we'll drop a marker to show where our diving area starts."

"What then?" Todd asked.

Rafael pointed to a chart.

"The first team will swim across the reef. They'll put markers on the reef's edge. The other team will follow in a Zodiac. A Zodiac is a twelve-foot inflatable boat. It can do many things the *Paz* can't," Rafael said. "If you see a wreck, come to the surface. We have big white floats to mark the spot."

"What about sharks?" Todd asked.

"Good question," Rafael said. "We'll bring the bang sticks down too."

When they were over the reef, Captain Sanchez slowed the *Paz*. Rafael threw the first marker over the side. It was anchored by a fifty-pound weight. It marked one end of Todd's five-mile stretch of reef.

Domingo put the Zodiac in the water. Jorge and Todd got in. Then Rafael and Franco dove in the water.

The reef was alive with life. Schools of fish swam by. Crabs walked around the coral.

For two hours Franco and Rafael swam across the reef. Then Rafael pointed to the surface. The diving teams switched places. Todd and Jorge went in the water. Franco and Rafael followed in the Zodiac.

Chapter 5

It was noon when Jorge and Todd
came up. Franco dropped another
marker. They would know where
they had stopped. Then Rafael drove
the Zodiac back to the *Paz*. It was
time for lunch.

Rafael could tell that Franco and
Todd were a little upset.

"Cheer up, guys. We haven't even
covered a quarter mile. Treasure

diving takes time," Rafael said. "And patience."

They spent the afternoon the same way as the morning. The results were the same too. No one saw a sunken ship.

In the next four days, they covered half of the salvage area. They didn't find anything. The fifth day was warm and sunny.

"Today's the day. I feel it!" Jorge said.

"I hope you're right," sighed Todd.

Franco was an hour into his morning dive. He swam to the edge of the reef. Something caught his eye. When he swam closer, he couldn't believe it. It was a huge mast with a mermaid on top!

Franco hoped it was part of a ship. It was! The ship was over one hundred feet long and lay on its side. Some of it was hanging off the edge of the reef. But it was still in Todd's salvage area. The ship was theirs!

The wreck was covered with sand, mud, and sea growth. It was hard to see. But it definitely was a ship. Franco found his dad and pointed toward it.

They both stared. Then they surfaced and waved to the Zodiac.

"Drop a marker here, Todd," Rafael said. "We're right over a wreck!"

Chapter 6

All four divers were thrilled.

"Todd and Jorge, put your gear on," Rafael said. "All four of us can get a closer look."

They anchored the Zodiac. Then Jorge and Todd got in the water. For fifteen minutes the four divers swam around the wreck. Then they went back to the Zodiac.

"Well, guys, what do you think?" Rafael asked.

"It's hard to tell," Jorge replied. "It's very dirty. I didn't see an opening."

"Neither did I," Rafael agreed. "I bet the opening is buried in the sand."

"I think you're right," Jorge replied. "We need to clean off some of that dirt!"

"Good idea," Rafael said. "Let's do it the quick way!"

Todd and Franco looked at each other. They didn't know what Rafael and Jorge were talking about.

"What do you mean by 'the quick way'?" Franco asked.

"We need to clean off the hull," Rafael said. "The fastest way to do it is with explosives."

"But we don't have explosives on the *Paz*," said Jorge. "So we need to go back to port."

It was one o'clock when they got back to the pier. Captain Sanchez ordered the explosives they needed.

The five of them dined at a local restaurant. Rafael liked talking to Captain Sanchez. He asked how the government protected the reef.

"All of our reefs are patrolled by navy gunboats," Captain Sanchez answered.

"But I haven't seen any," Rafael replied.

"You were too busy diving," the captain said. "They were out there."

Four men were eating dinner on the other side of the restaurant.

One of them looked up. "Look at Sanchez with his American friends," he said.

"Have they found anything yet?" another one asked.

"No," a third man answered. "They're still looking around the reef. But I'm keeping an eye on them. If they find something, I'll know."

"Good," replied the first man. "If they find something, we'll give them four days to get the treasure. Then we'll pay the *Paz* a visit. The government can stop us from diving on the reef. But they can't stop us from stealing from those who do."

All four men laughed.

At dawn the *Paz* was off again. This time they anchored next to the wreck. They didn't need the Zodiac anymore. Now they'd dive from the deck of the *Paz*.

The four divers set up the explosives. A small blast would clean off the hull.

A rumble could be heard from the reef. Thousands of bubbles floated up to the surface.

"There's no hurry to get down there," Jorge said. "We won't be able to see much now."

When the water was clear, the four divers jumped in. They studied the wreck. The explosives had cleared away a lot of the sea growth.

Now they could see the hull. After twenty minutes, Rafael signaled for the group to surface.

"So far so good," Franco said. "What do we do now?"

"The valuables on these old ships were kept in storage. We'll get to it through an opening in the hull. But the opening in this hull is buried," Rafael said. "So we have to make our own hole."

"With explosives?" Todd asked.

"You got that right," Jorge answered.

Chapter 7

Rafael and Jorge talked with
Captain Sanchez about what to do
next. They finally had a plan.

"We're going to make a five-foot
hole in the hull," Rafael explained.
"The blast has to be big enough to do
it. But it can't be too big. Or it will
damage the wreck. So we have to be
careful."

An hour later Rafael and Jorge set up the explosives. They put them on the front of the hull. They swam back to the *Paz* when they were finished. Once again there was a dull roar when the explosives went off. A few pieces of wood from the hull floated to the surface.

"Looks good!" Jorge exclaimed.

"When we enter the hull, we have to be careful," said Rafael. "Every diver has to tie a safety line around his waist. You can get lost inside. This line will help someone find you."

"Won't it be really dark?" asked Todd.

"Yes," Rafael replied. "We'll use underwater lights. Todd, why don't you and Jorge go down first?"

Everyone was excited to look around the ship.

Jorge and Todd jumped in the water. Their safety lines were behind them. Each line was tied to a post on the *Paz*. The huge wreck lay in front of them. They looked at the hole in the hull. Todd saw a lot of dead fish from the explosion.

Todd heard a strange creaking sound. The ship was shifting in the current. Both men entered the hull. It was small and dark. Then Todd looked behind him. Jorge was gone!

Todd shined his light around the ship. Finally he saw Jorge's safety line. He followed it down a passageway. Jorge was in another room. He was trying to open a big trunk. Jorge gave Todd his light. Then he used both hands to pull open the trunk.

It was filled with gold coins! Jorge took a handful of coins and put them in his pocket. Then he motioned for Todd to go to the surface. They used their safety lines to find their way.

Just outside the hull was a huge shark! It was a twenty-foot-long great white. The dead fish must have attracted it. Now the shark was in a feeding frenzy!

Chapter 8

If Jorge and Todd left the ship, the shark could attack. But they couldn't stay for long. They only had forty-five minutes of air left. They had to let the *Paz* know they had a problem.

Jorge had an idea. He grabbed his safety line. Then he started jerking it. He hoped Rafael would see it. Then Rafael would realize something was wrong.

Domingo saw the line moving.

"Look! Señor Silva!" Domingo shouted. "Why are they pulling on the safety line?"

"Something must be wrong," Rafael said. "I'd better have a look."

Rafael jumped in the water. He came up a minute later.

"There's a huge shark down there. Pass me the bang sticks," Rafael yelled.

"How many do you want?" Franco asked.

"Two," Rafael said. "That's one big fish!"

Rafael had a bang stick in each hand. He headed back down. When he reached the wreck, he saw the shark. It was forty yards away.

Rafael entered the hull. He handed Jorge a bang stick. All three divers swam for the surface.

They hadn't gone ten feet when the shark saw them. It turned to attack. It swam toward them very fast. They knew they couldn't outrun the shark. So they turned to face it.

The three men were breathing hard. The great white seemed to slow down. Was it grinning at them? Its white teeth shined in the water. Then it turned up its nose and swam away. The three divers didn't know why. Maybe they weren't worth the effort.

Back on the *Paz*, Todd told the others about the shark.

"You guys have all the fun! I never even saw the shark," Franco said.

Jorge almost forgot about the coins in his pocket. He pulled out the gold.

"Congratulations!" Captain Sanchez said. "It looks like you found a real treasure."

"I know," Jorge said. "But I'm concerned about the ship."

"What do you mean?" the captain asked.

"The wreck is hanging off the reef," Jorge replied. "It's moving with the current. I'm afraid it will fall."

"*What?*" Todd asked. "Could the whole ship slide off the reef into deep water?"

"Yes," Jorge said. "And if it fell with a diver inside, he'd be gone too."

"But the wreck has been there over a hundred years. Why would it fall now?" Franco asked.

"We've used a lot of explosives," Rafael said. "We must have moved it. But let's dive while we still can. Franco, are you ready?"

"You bet!" Franco said.

Domingo lowered a steel mesh container into the water. It was right next to the wreck. Then Rafael and Franco jumped in. Hopefully they would fill it up with gold!

Chapter 9

Rafael and Franco swam into the ship. Soon they got to the trunk filled with gold. They put gold coins into the mesh container for almost two hours. It was tough work.

For the next three days, the divers worked hard. It took a long time to salvage sunken treasure.

"How much do you think we have so far?" Todd asked.

"It's hard to tell," Captain Sanchez said. "But I'd guess you have about a million dollars in gold. Maybe more."

"Wow!" Todd exclaimed. "And there's still a lot down there!"

"Yes," Captain Sanchez said. "You may have one the biggest treasures ever found on these reefs."

Back in Guayaquil, four men stood on the docks. They talked about the *Paz*.

"They must have found something," one of the men said. "They haven't moved in four days."

"All right," said another man. "Let's hit them tonight. Meet back here at midnight. We can be at the reef by two in the morning. They'll all be asleep by then."

In the middle of the night, the four men anchored their boat a few feet from the *Paz*. They lowered a Zodiac into the water.

Everyone on the *Paz* was sleeping.

Amigo heard something. He let out a growl that woke Captain Sanchez. Amigo never growled. Something must be wrong. The captain went to check it out. There was someone on deck! Captain Sanchez grabbed a gun. Then he turned the lights on.

The four robbers were caught by surprise. One fired a shot. Captain Sanchez fired back. His bullet hit the man in the leg.

The noise woke up everyone else. They raced onto the deck. When they saw what was happening, they helped stop the robbers.

"What do we do now?" Jorge asked. "Will the police pick these guys up?"

"They would," Captain Sanchez replied. "But we got a storm warning. Bad weather is going to hit tomorrow. I was going to take us back to Guayaquil. But since we're all awake, we might as well go now."

They tied up the robbers. By daylight they were docked in Guayaquil.

Chapter 10

The police were at the dock. They
arrested the four robbers.

That afternoon the storm hit.
It was very bad. But by noon the
next day, it was over. The wind
had stopped. The sun was shining.
Captain Sanchez thought it was safe
to take the *Paz* back out. Thanks to
Amigo, all the gold was still on board.

They went back to the wreck site.

Rafael and Franco dove under to check on the ship. It was hard to see. The storm had made the water murky. Rafael and Franco could not find the wreck. They swam to where the ship had been. It was gone. All that was left was the huge mast with the mermaid. The rest of the ship had fallen off the reef. It was again lost at sea.

Rafael and Franco swam back to the *Paz*. They shared the bad news.

"The ship fell off the reef during the storm," Rafael said. "It's lost forever."

Everyone was both happy and sad. They were happy that they found the wreck and the treasure. But they were sad that the rest of the gold slipped through their hands.

The Ecuadorian government reviewed the treasure. It was worth a million dollars. They kept half. They gave Todd Bardo Jr. a check for five hundred thousand dollars.

"Okay, Todd. Our expenses were sixty thousand," Rafael said. "And I think we should tip Captain Sanchez, Domingo, and Amigo fifteen grand. That leaves us with four hundred twenty-five thousand to share. Todd, you get fifty-five percent. That comes to two hundred thirty-three thousand. Jorge, Franco, and I get sixty-three thousand dollars each."

"Wow!" Todd exclaimed. "That's a lot of money. But I can't help thinking about the millions that got away."

"You're right about that," said Rafael. "But you have to think about the treasure you *did* find. You are over two hundred thousand dollars richer. Not bad for a few days' work!"

"True," Todd said. "And thank you for making this happen. I never could have done this on my own."

"No problem, Todd. I'm glad I helped! I'm sure your dad would be very proud of you too," said Rafael.

"I bet he would be," Todd said. "I'm going to donate some of this treasure to his clinic. I think he would have wanted that. And, Franco, speaking of fathers, you got a great one. You're lucky to have him."

"I know," Franco said. "He's the best!"